Fra<

MW01143959

About This Book

Title: *Will's Bike*

Step: 4

Word Count: 122

Skills in Focus: Silent 'e'

Tricky Words: learn, right

Ideas for Using this Book

Before Reading:
- **Comprehension:** Ask the reader what they think the book may be about. Prompt them to explain their thinking based on evidence from the cover and any relevant background knowledge.
- **Phonics:** Write the word *bike* on the board. Explain that the word *bike* has a silent e at the end. Point to the pattern, i.e. Explain that this is the vowel-consonant-e pattern. The silent e makes the vowel before it have a long sound, saying its own name. Explain that in the word *bike*, the silent e makes the i say /ī/. Ask the reader to help think of other words that have a silent e. Model how to recognize and sound out these words (examples from the book include: drive, ride, home, shade, take).

During Reading:
- Have the reader point under each word as they read it.
- **Decoding:** If stuck on a word, help readers say each sound and blend it together smoothly.
- **Comprehension:** Ask the reader to infer how characters may be feeling at different points. Prompt them to back up their ideas with evidence from the text!

After Reading:
Discuss the book. Some ideas for questions:
- Where did the family go in the story? Why did they go there?
- How do you think Will felt when he found the red bike that was just his size? How do you know?

Will's Bike

Text by Leanna Koch
Educational content by Kristen Cowen
Illustrated by Andy Rowland

PICTURE WINDOW BOOKS
a capstone imprint

This is Dad. This is
Mom. This is Will.

WILL

5

Mom, Dad, and Will take
a drive to the bike shop.

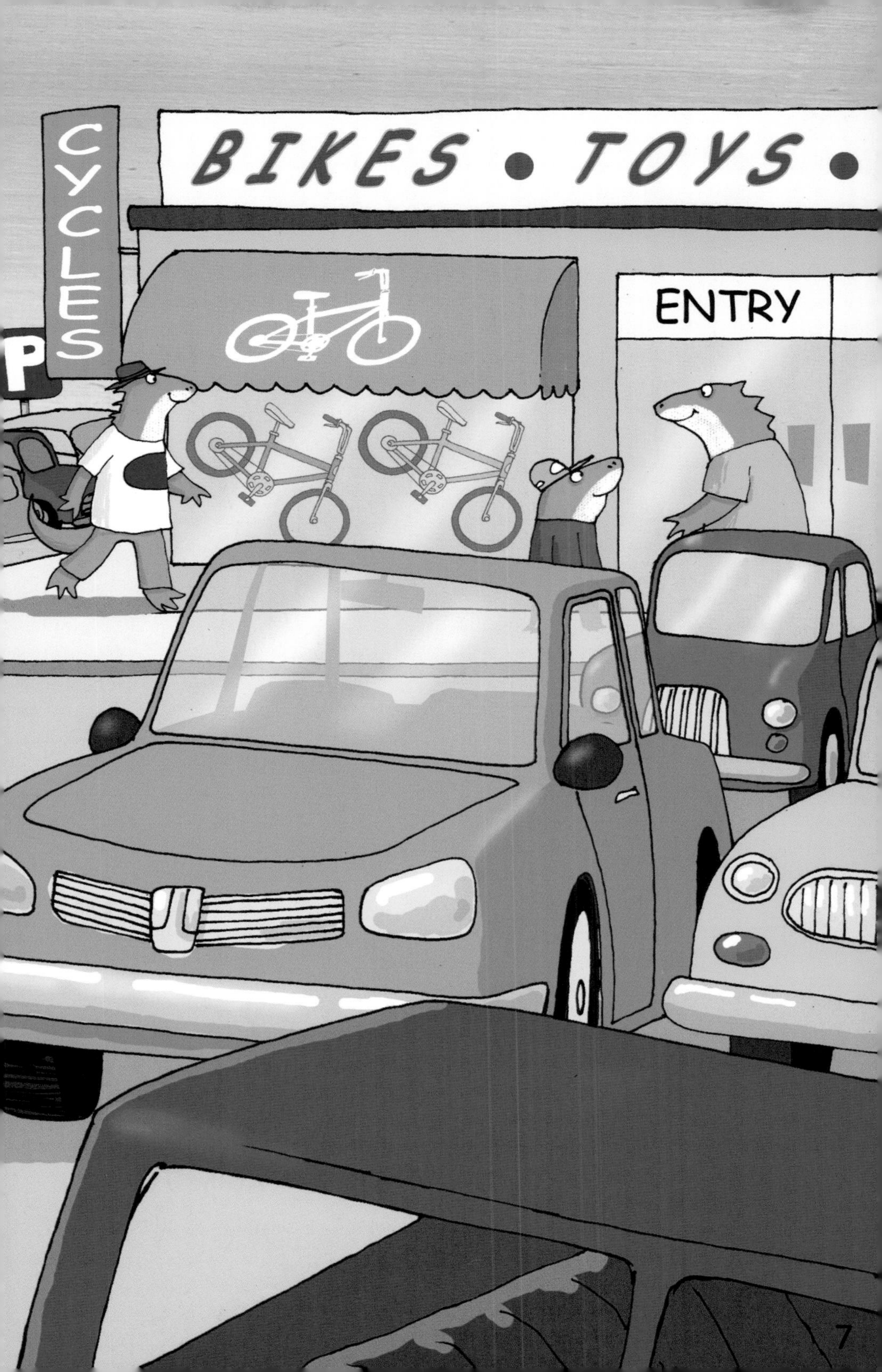
CYCLES
BIKES • TOYS •
ENTRY
P

"It is time to learn to ride
a bike, Will," Mom says.

ENTRY

9

"These bikes are on sale."

"I came here to pick a bike," says Will, "but I like all of these bikes."

"This bike is nice," says Dad.

15

Will is scared. "This bike is too big," said Dad.

"Trikes are nice," says Mom.

WHEELS

"That bike is not the right size," Dad says.

"That bike is a nice shade of red," says Mom. "Is it the right size?"

Will smiles.

The red bike is just Will's size.

27

"We will take the red bike,"
says Will's dad.

29

Will can ride his bike home.

More Ideas:

Writing with silent e words:
Challenge yourself to write a story using as many words as possible that have the silent e. Your story can be as silly or serious as you want!

Here is a list of some of the silent e words from this story: bike, drive, home, ride, shade, take

Extended Learning Activity

Writing Prompt

My Perfect Bike
Think about what your perfect, dream bike would look like. Would it be red like Will's? How many wheels would it have? Use as many adjectives, or describing words, as you can to write about your perfect, dream bike. Then, share where you would like to ride your perfect bike.

Published by Picture Window Books,
an imprint of Capstone
1710 Roe Crest Drive,
North Mankato, Minnesota 56003
capstonepub.com

Will's Bike was originally published as
Little Lizard's New Bike, copyright 2011 by Stone Arch Books.

Library of Congress Cataloging-in-Publication Data is available
on the Library of Congress website.

ISBN: 9780756594862 (hardback)
ISBN: 9780756583644 (paperback)
ISBN: 9780756583620 (eBook PDF)

Printed and bound in the USA. 5757